Peppa Pig™

Mr Fox's Shop

Mummy and Daddy Pig are wrapping up a present for
Granny and Grandpa Pig's wedding anniversary.
It's a glass vase.

"That's a bit of a boring present," says Peppa.
"Ho, ho!" laughs Daddy Pig. "It's a present
for grown-ups."

Peppa and George want to buy Granny and Grandpa Pig a present, too. George gets their piggy bank to see how much money they have.

"We have one penny and two buttons to spend," says Peppa.

Peppa, George, Mummy and Daddy Pig head to Mr Fox's shop with the piggy bank. Peppa is very excited about buying Granny and Grandpa Pig a present.

When they arrive, they open Mr Fox's shop
door and a bell rings. Ting-a-ling-ling!

"Hello there!" says Mr Fox from behind
the shop counter. "Can I help you?"
"It's Granny and Grandpa Pig's wedding
anniversary," says Mummy Pig.

"They are both very old and
need a present," explains Peppa.
"My shop has everything," replies Mr Fox.
"I'm sure you'll find something."

"A big teddy!" cries Peppa, picking
a teddy bear from the shelf.
"I love it. This can be the present!"

"The present is not for you," says Mummy Pig.
"It's for Granny and Grandpa!"
"Oh, yes," says Peppa, disappointed.

"Do your granny and grandpa like digging in the garden?" asks Mr Fox.
"Yes," replies Peppa.

"Then why not get them a bucket and
spade each?" asks Mr Fox.
"They have spades and buckets, and forks,
and everything!" says Peppa.

"I know!" cries Peppa. "Grandpa likes sailing his boat!"
"Say no more," says Mr Fox. "I have everything
a sailor could wish for!"

"Do you have pirates' treasure?" asks Peppa.
"Ah," sighs Mr Fox. "Everything *except* pirates' treasure."
"Oh," Peppa and George sigh, disappointed.

"How about this plastic oak chair?" suggests Mr Fox.
"Is it comfortable?" asks Daddy Pig.
"You can't sit on it!" warns Mr Fox. "You just
look at it, because it looks nice."

"That's not much fun," says Peppa.
"Even for a grown-up."

"My shop sells everything," says Mr Fox.
"There must be something you like?"
"There is!" cries Peppa, picking up the teddy bear again.

"I like this teddy, and I think
Granny and Grandpa would like it, too."
"Ho, ho!" laughs Daddy Pig. "Let's buy the teddy, then."

"A very good choice!" says Mr Fox.
"Who's going to pay?"
George empties the piggy bank on to the shop counter.

"One penny and two buttons," says Mr Fox. "Here's your change — one button."
"Thank you, Mr Fox," replies Peppa.
Then, Peppa and her family head to Granny and Grandpa's house.

"Happy anniversary!" cheers Mummy Pig,
as Granny opens the vase.
"Oh, another glass vase," says Grandpa, not very excited.
"It's a grown-up present," says Peppa.
"That's why it's a bit boring."

Then, Granny opens the present from Peppa and George. "A teddy bear!" she says, delighted. "Thank you, Peppa and George. It's the best present we've ever had!" "Indeed!" says Grandpa excitedly!